I0663060

DAMMIT!

A Book of Short Stories,
Musings and Commentaries
to Make You Laugh and Cry

Written by
Thomas L. Rose

CCB Publishing
British Columbia, Canada

Dammit!: A Book of Short Stories, Musings
and Commentaries to Make You Laugh and Cry

Copyright ©2025 by Thomas L. Rose
ISBN-13 978-1-77143-619-9
First Edition

Library and Archives Canada Cataloguing in Publication
Title: Dammit! : a book of short stories, musings and commentaries to make
you laugh and cry / by Thomas L. Rose.
Names: Rose, Thomas L., 1940- author.
Issued in print and electronic formats.
ISBN 9781771436199 (softcover) – ISBN 9781771436205 (PDF)
Additional cataloguing data available from Library and Archives Canada

Cover artwork credit: Original cover design by Brock T. Rose.
Permission statement: Permission to use image(s) and references to PinonyHead
              Doll (Dammit Doll) courtesy of Marie Adame from
              La Dame Creates (www.ladamecreates.com).

Publisher: CCB Publishing
             British Columbia, Canada
             www.ccbpublishing.com

Dedicated
to all my friends and family who have
encouraged my new writing career.

*"Nothing on this earth
is more prized than true friendship."*
- Thomas Aquinas

Books by Thomas L. Rose

Balloon in A Box: Coping with Grief

Dammit!
A Book of Short Stories, Musings and
Commentaries to Make You Laugh and Cry

The Secret is in the Pasta
A Murder Mystery Novel

Cooking Together Chinese Style

Cooking Together Quick and Easy

Cooking Together Revisited

Contents

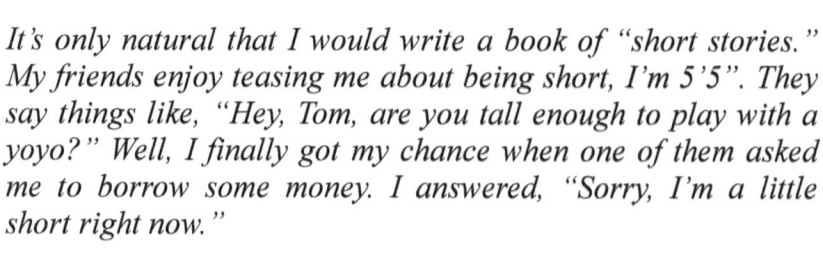

It's only natural that I would write a book of "short stories." My friends enjoy teasing me about being short, I'm 5'5". They say things like, "Hey, Tom, are you tall enough to play with a yoyo?" Well, I finally got my chance when one of them asked me to borrow some money. I answered, "Sorry, I'm a little short right now."

Dammit or if you prefer:
Nuts, Egad!, Boulder Dash, Bloody Hell, Fiddle Sticks, Blimey,
Drat, Heck, Oh My, Gadzooks!, Sheesh, Dang, Uh-Oh,
Yikes or as the Englishman would say, Bugger.

My wife just called me asking if we had any moving boxes at work. I told her no... All of our boxes are still. That's why we purchased them from a stationary store.

Moving Again

Dammit, I hate moving, but here I am doing it again. My first move was to my apartment after college for my new job. Then came our first house when Jill and I got married, and then two more times with her because with family, we needed more space. And then came my bachelor pad when she took me out after 20 years and three houses. She, of course, got to keep the last home.

My next move was with the second wife, Susie; she had always wanted to live beside a lake, so we bought a cute little cottage with blue shutters and a nice white pier with a flag post. She also talked me into buying a pontoon boat, explaining how we would take romantic sunset cruises. That marriage lasted precisely one year, meaning I enjoyed one season of romantic cruises. Of course, she got the cottage and the boat. And I was again moving into another bachelor pad.

I am now married to Nancy and moving again into a villa on the golf course. Nancy thought it would be nice since I like to play golf. So far, it has been going very well. The place still needs some remodeling and decorating, so we decided to save money and are doing most of the remodeling and decorating ourselves. It could be a mistake, but…

It's a very nice middle-class neighborhood. There are 75 units (villas) in the complex. There is a clubhouse, swimming pool and pickleball courts, which Nancy insists we learn to play once we get settled. The neighbors, Joe and Carol, are lovely, as are all the others we have met. Joe and Carol like to drink wine, and better yet, they like to share. Everyone seems to have a dog, as there is often a parade of dog walkers in front of our house. And, of course, Nancy thinks maybe we should consider getting a dog too. About 50% of the people in the neighborhood are either widows or widowers. There is one elderly gentleman, I'm told his name is Wilson, and he is hard of hearing. He walks by twice daily, morning and afternoon, and always nods and says, "Good day," not stopping, just continuing his journey.

Speaking of settling, as I said, things are going pretty well, but the other day, Nancy sprung it on me that she wants to build a table for the kitchen/dining area. Can I make a table? Well, I took a wood working class in high school 35 years ago! Check out her design: As you can see, it comes out from a corner but also must be able to move to the center of the room when needed. Suppose the table is 36" wide and 48" long (not including the triangle piece). When purchasing lumber, I am buying an 8-foot piece of good birch, which she wants to finish with a walnut color. I also need four 4"x4" posts for the legs.

Nancy and I have been living here for about six weeks, during and after our remodeling, painting, etc. One side of the garage is full of boxes of our stuff, mostly hers. The other side contains all the supplies for the remodeling, including all my new tools. The lumber for the table is stacked on two sawhorses, and the plans are attached. Occasionally, I stop and look at the drawing, thinking I should start the project, but I have yet to figure out the dimensions of the triangular piece. Knowing that the one dimension is 36", what should the other sides be to fit correctly? There is a formula, but what is it?

When I arrived home from work today, Nancy told me that she had the garage door open and saw Wilson looking at my table project, but by the time she could get out to the garage, he was gone. That's interesting. I need to talk with him the next time he walks by. He could be a carpenter and help me with the project.

Nancy said that Joe and Carol had invited us for cocktail hour at 5:30, so I quickly changed into comfortable clothes and grabbed a bottle of wine. Nancy had made some cream cheese roll-ups, and we headed to their deck. Joe always had a few good jokes for us, usually about marriage, and today was no different:

How is a wife like bacon?

-They both look, smell, and taste amazing. They also both slowly kill you.

What do a wife and a grenade have in common?

-They both leave you in pain when you pull off the ring.

One glass of wine turned into several, and the sun had set over the 14th green. Nancy and I said our goodbyes, promising the next time it would be on our deck. At 9:00, neither of us was hungry, so we split a donut and headed to bed. I told her I had an early appointment and would get up early. She commented that it was good because she had a plumber coming early to hook up the plumbing for the remodeled guest bath. I am only a plumber if you want an indoor swimming pool.

Arriving home the following evening, I changed clothes, poured a glass of wine, *to help me figure out the corner measurements,* and headed to the garage to tackle the table project. Looking down at the plans I had taped to the lumber, I saw a note that read, "Pythagorean Theorem, young man." I

3

remember this, but what did it mean here, and who had written the note? I immediately ran to the computer and typed in the search, "Pythagorean Theorem," and up it came, "The Pythagoras Theorem holds $a^2 + b^2 = c^2$. Yes, it gave me the formula to compute the dimensions I needed.

Going to bed that evening, I explained it to Nancy, still wondering who had written the note. Nancy suggested it might have been Wilson. As I snuggled with her, I believed Wilson had left the note. Please wait a minute; his first name is not Wilson, his last name is Wilson, Bob Wilson, my algebra teacher in high school. He always said, "Young man, someday you will use what you learn here."

I wonder if the "Pythagorean Theorem" works for marriage because, dammit, I never want to move again.

Excellent After All This Time

They were getting ready to move, so the wife began cleaning out her husband's desk. As she went through the papers, she noticed an old, yellowed receipt: "Miller's Shoe Repair." Looking more closely at the receipt, she realized it was for a pair of shoes he had dropped off twenty years ago and forgot to pick up.

She picked up the phone, wondering if they are still in business, dials the number, and is shocked when a woman answers, "Millers shoe repair!"

"Hello! Oh my, I can't believe you're still in business! Look, I'm calling about an ancient shoe repair receipt, receipt #24789."

"Let me look," the woman says. There's a long pause, and then she comes back on the line. "Johnson?" she says. "Is that correct?

"Yes," the wife replies, "that's my husband, Fred Johnson!"

"A pair of black size ten dress shoes?"

"Yes, that would be the correct size. That's amazing! After all this time, you fixed and kept his shoes for twenty years! Can I come over now and pick them up?"

There's a pause on the other end of the line. "They'll be ready two weeks from Tuesday." CLICK

Dammit!

I knew a fortune teller once, but all he could predict was winter weather until he found out the magic shop had sold him a snow globe instead of a crystal ball.

The Medium

I'm not sure why I am doing this, but my friend Betty swears this lady is real. Of course, Betty believes in Santa Claus, the Tooth Fairy, and the Easter Bunny. Also, black cats and the number thirteen are unlucky, and four-leaf clovers and a rabbit's foot will bring you good luck. She also lives by her astrological sign; she is a Pisces, representing the constant division of attention between fantasy and reality. She continually reminds me that my sign is Taurus, an earth sign represented by the bull. Like our celestial spirit animal, we enjoy relaxing in serene, rustic environments, surrounded by soft sounds, soothing aromas, succulent flavors, and ruled by Venus. This enchanting planet governs love, beauty, and money... that's me.

My name is Jill Bower, and my husband is Nick Bower, a member of a Special Forces unit that was stationed in Afghanistan. He was killed in a raid on a Taliban stronghold in the mountains. It has been three years since I opened the door, finding an officer to give me the bad news that Nick was missing in action, and then three weeks later, when he was confirmed dead. I think of him every day, and my grief journey continues to move on day after day. Betty has been my rock and talked me into this encounter with Madame Selene because she had made contact with her father, allowing Betty to speak with him. She is convinced that Madame Selene can do the same for me with Nick.

So there I stood, at her door which had a sign that read: "Madame Selene where Visions are Unveiled." The house was in one of our town's old neighborhoods, with homes dating back to the 1800s, and they are all well-maintained. The porch light was on, I could see the brick had been restored, and the white trim was relatively newly painted. Spring flowers surrounded the house, including a porch swing, table, and two chairs. The home looked like all the others in the neighborhood, not particularly the home of a psychic who could communicate with the dead.

I rang the bell and heard a sequence of lovely bells. As expected, she opened the door wearing a full-length striped dress with a matching scarf around her head. I was expecting an older woman, but Madame Selene was a very good looking younger woman in her early to mid-thirties. She had beautiful, deep blue eyes accented by eyeliner. Funny, though, she was wearing red flip flops.

Her greeting was warm and pleasant as she invited me into the house. As I followed her down the hall, I saw that the furnishings in the home were from the late 1800s or early 1900s. I was drawn to the high ceiling and ornate chandelier as we entered the living room. I commented on how much I liked it, and she explained that it and most of the furnishings had been passed down over the generations. She also mentioned that her ancestors had built the home in the 1860s. The only changes were heating, air conditioning, electrical, carpet, and fresh paint. Every generation had also added some additional furniture pieces and paintings.

Even though it had been a warm spring day, there was a low burning fire in the large stone fireplace, a real wood fire. There was an old grandfather clock against one wall and a candelabra with six lit candles on the mantle. The open window at the room's far end created a soft breeze. A small ornate lamp on an end table, the fireplace, candles, and what was left of the evening daylight gave the room a warm, comfortable feeling. I assumed this is what was needed to create the proper mood for a séance for contacting those on the other side.

She pointed for me to sit on the sofa and took the seat across from me in a high back winged chair. Between us was a coffee table containing two carafes, two cups and saucers, sugar, and cream, and she explained that one was coffee and the other tea. I selected black coffee, which she poured and handed to me. She said, "Betty told me about your husband, that he was killed serving his country, a real hero. His name was Nick, correct?"

"Yes, Captain Nick Bower, U.S. Special Forces," I responded.

"Well, Jill, we will try to reach Nick on the other side. Sometimes, it isn't easy based on the relationship you had. Talking with Betty, I understand you and Nick had a strong, loving relationship."

I wondered what else Betty had told her?

"Which means I am sure we can make contact." Reaching across the table and taking my hands, she said, "Just sit back and relax."

Madame Selene closed her eyes and began to chant softly, "Captain Bower, Nick, can you come through to me? Your wife, Jill, is here and would like to speak with you."

The grandfather clock was ticking, time was passing, and nothing seemed to be happening. Then suddenly, she let out a deep breath, opened her eyes, and appeared to be looking past me into space. Then her eyes closed, and the fireplace ember cracked and flashed; the lamp dimmed and brightened while the drapes rustled softly with the breeze.

"Jill, I feel fear in your hands; please do not be afraid. I am sure Nick will always protect you from evil."

Again, she let out a deep breath, opening her eyes with that same distance from before. Only now, her lips began to move, and out came a voice much different than Madame Selene's. It was deeper and sounded very distant. *Could it be Nick?* The voice was garbled and impossible to understand with the volume flowing up and down.

Selene asked, "Captain Nick Bower, is that you?" Again, I could only hear a voice that is impossible to understand. "Captain, please come through; your wife Jill is here with me."

Then it happens, I hear Nick. "Jill, this is Nick. I love you very much and am always here to protect and guide you. Get the hell out of there; Madame Selene is a fake." I was frozen in my seat, and I couldn't move. I heard Nick say, "Jill, leave immediately before she awakens. The woman is a fake... get out... Move now!!"

I managed to gain my senses, grabbed my purse, and ran out the door to my car down the road.

Now here I am in my driveway, not remembering how I got here. I rush into the house, lock the door, and throw myself on the couch.

What the hell just happened? Did I hear Nick? If Madame Selene is fake, how did I hear Nick? If she was a fake, why would she tell me to leave? Dammit, what the hell just happened??

Psychic's Advice

A woman went to a psychic and found out she was going to live to be 100!

She figured if she was going to be around that long, she may as well look her best. She got the works! Facelift, breast enhancement, nose job and looked amazing!

After her final procedure she got hit by a bus and died.

Upon arriving at the pearly gates she cried and cried! "I was supposed to live 40 more years!"

Saint Peter said, "Oh, sorry, I didn't recognize you."

Dammit!

The Devil You Say

Damn, I think I accidentally summoned the devil. Yea, really... last night, I had a dream that I was very angry with my present position in life. I was cursing God and blaming him for my misfortune. I had lost my job, a very good one in a prominent investment firm, earning six figures. My ex-wife had, as they say, "taken me to the cleaners," getting everything I had in the divorce. Now I had no job, no six-figure income, no money, and creditors calling and emailing constantly. My girlfriend just broke up with me for another guy, who is a good friend. I have no friends, and my family no longer speaks to me. Life sucks!!

In my dream, I was walking down this lonely road. It was windy and foggy, and I was cold. Suddenly this guy was standing alongside the road. He was dressed in a costly and flashy suit, his tie looked on fire, and he had a topcoat over one arm. He was smoking a big cigar and holding an excellent brandy bottle.

He asked if I would like a "pull" off the bottle and a cigar. I accepted. The brandy made me feel warm, and the cigar was the best I had ever smoked. He told me an old Cuban gentleman made them special for him. He asked if he could walk with me because we seemed to be headed in the same direction; I told him I didn't know where I was going, and we started walking. He said I looked cold and gave me his coat, which I pulled over my shoulders. It made me feel warm but strange. He commented that he thought I looked exhausted, confused, and sad. I told him that he was correct. He asked me to explain, so I told him my story. As we walked and I talked, we continued to share the bottle and smoke our cigars. He was absorbing and very attentive to my story. He seemed, by his questions, to know what I would say.

We had walked for a considerable time, and the scenery never changed. It was the same cold, foggy, and lonely road with no houses, bare trees, long grass, and dark gray clouds. We finally reached a fork in the road with an old wooden bench. He suggested we sit and rest, and he told me how sorry he was for all my difficulties. He then told me that he had a lot of important contacts and maybe he could help me find a job. I told him it would be great and that I would appreciate any opportunity, that I was "at the end of my rope" and would do anything for a job. He said, "Son, sometimes in life, that is necessary." He said he felt that everything would work out with my other problems. I said, "From your lips to God's ears." With that, he stepped back quickly, shook his head, told me I should take the road to the right, and promptly turned down the left lane. I hollered after him that he didn't know how to contact me if he could get me a job interview. He shouted back that he knew how to reach me and would see me soon, then disappeared into the fog. I was confused; I hadn't told him how to contact me. What did he mean he would see me again?? At this point, I was awakened by my alarm.

I sat on the edge of my bed for a long time, trying to make sense of the dream. I finally moved on to fix myself a cup of coffee and watch the morning news, still confused by the dream.

The phone rang; it was the human resource department of a company to which I had sent a job application and resume. The gentleman said they had reviewed my information and wanted to offer me a job. He said the salary range would be about 20%

higher than my previous job. He asked if I could come to their offices in two days at 10:00, when they would present me with the offer. Of course, I gave him a positive response. I could hardly believe what had just happened. To celebrate, I decided to get dressed and treat myself to an excellent breakfast at my favorite restaurant. While eating, I received a phone call from my lawyer saying that he had appealed to the judge who had presided over the divorce, that he was willing to review the financial arrangements, and that my loss may be considerably less than initially set. He said he would contact me for lunch in the next few days after he had closed the deal. So far, it had been a day of surprises. It was all good!

After breakfast, I went to the bank, cashed my last IRA, transferred it to my checking account, and proceeded to shop for a new suit for the job interview. At my favorite men's store, I purchased a new gray suit, shirt, and tie to match, along with some new gray shoes. I had my car washed and cleaned inside. By then, it was time for lunch, lobster bisque, and a glass of champagne at the country club.

I arrived back home at about 2:30 pm, grabbing my mail. There, of course, were more past due bills and an invitation, probably someone's wedding. I decided that since I had transferred the IRA, I might pay the bills, but first, let's check the invitation. Unbelievable, it's an invitation to a family reunion in two months!! After paying all of my bills, I sat back in my recliner and began to reflect on the unreal day I had experienced when the phone rang. It was an old girlfriend who called, saying she was in town and was available for dinner. I told her I would pick her up at her hotel and then make reservations at the best restaurant in the city. We had a wonderful time—sharing old times and a couple of bottles of fine wine. We returned to the hotel and her room for a nightcap. And, well, a "gentleman does not kiss and tell."

Driving home, I kept thinking about my unreal day, but why question my good fortune? Just go with it. Arriving home "very late," I realized the clothes I purchased still hung in the back of the car. I grabbed them and, once in the house, went directly to the closet, hanging the suit and shirt in their proper places. I took the tie to hang on the rack and said, "What the hell?" Hanging there was a fiery tie just like the gentleman in my dream was wearing!! Dammit, what have I done!!

We should never think that the devil does not exist,
that is when he is most pleased and powerful.

Dammit!

Proverb 20:29:
"The glory of the young is their strength,
but the beauty of the aged is their grey hair."

What Did You Say?

Oh dammit, where are my hearing aids? They were very expensive, over $5,000, and the kids insisted I get the model you can control with your cell phone. I put it off for as long as possible, but I gave in when my hearing was at about 60%. It's hell to get old and forgetful. I seem to lose things daily.

If I don't shape up, my son will put me in the "home." Now let me see where my phone is, and I will call him to help find them. Hell, now I can't find my phone!! The family gave me one of those Google things so I could say, "Google find my phone," and a lovely lady would tell me, "Your phone is now ringing." But without my hearing aids, I couldn't hear her or my phone. "Google" can give you a lot of information if you ask. It can also be an alarm clock, but I don't sleep with my hearing aids in, so I can't hear it. What a vicious circle; it's hell to get old.

If I can find my phone, I can call my son, Bradley, who will help me find my hearing aids for the umpteenth time. My son is a great kid, and I love him very much, along with his wife Rachel and the grandkids Tammy and Tommy. *(Tammy is about to make me a great-grandfather.)* But I know Rachel thinks Brad spends too much time looking after me and that it might be time for the retirement home. I need to stop losing and forgetting things and maybe she will change her mind.

Okay, I need to concentrate on finding my phone. Let's see, the last time I used it was in the car last night driving home from Rocco's Bistro. I met friends there for an early dinner, senior rates from 4:30 to 6:00. We sat talking about "the good old days" until almost 8:00. I had called Brad to let him know I was on my way home from the restaurant. He always worries if I am driving after dark. Okay, I checked the car, the phone is not on the dash, in the cell phone holder, or under the seat. So I would carry the phone through the back door into the kitchen, checking the kitchen counters, but there was no phone. Next, I would have gone to the closet and changed clothes, into my pajamas. No phone in the closet. I was tired but sat at my desk and checked my emails—no phone. I went to bed and turned on the TV news—no phone on the bed table or in the bed and no hearing aids. Oh yeah, I brushed my teeth and took my pills. It's the same story: no phone or hearing aids in the bathroom. Damn, damn, dammit!!

I have spent a lot of time on my search, and I am hungry. I haven't even had my coffee yet. So, it's time to make breakfast and a cup of coffee in the Keurig thing the kids bought me for Christmas. Oh yeah, I need to add those pods to my grocery list, or I will forget to buy any. I will have hash browns, two eggs, and a sausage patty with a slice of whole wheat toast. Oops, no sausage. I better add that to the grocery list. I guess it will be bacon. Wait, what's lying on top of that white Styrofoam container... it's my phone. That's right, I brought home leftover food from the restaurant and put it in the refrigerator along with my phone. Well, one down... one to go!!

Okay, I finished breakfast and my coffee. I will clean up the kitchen later. First, let's try another search for hearing aids. I always place my hearing aids in the cup on the bathroom counter or the bed table if I use them while watching TV before bed. They are not in the bathroom cup, on the counter, or on the floor. They're not in the bed table cup either, so let's move the table and see if they are on the floor anywhere around it; no luck. *Note to me, "I need to clean behind the bed table because there are lots of chips and peanuts, etc.*" Okay, the last hope is to check the bed carefully while making it; no hearing aids.

Let's clean the kitchen from breakfast, and maybe I will have a "hearing aid vision." Dishes are in the dishwasher, food is in the refrigerator, and it's 10:30 am. Now what? Why don't I sit down, listen to music on the CD player, oops no hearing aids so maybe I'll just read a little, and think, and maybe the "hearing aid vision" will occur?

Wow, it's 12:30, I must have dozed off, and a hearing aid dream didn't happen. I can't put it off any longer. I need to call Brad. Damn, I hate this!!

"Hello, Brad, it's the 'ole man' and I need your help. I lost my hearing aids."

"Dammit, Dad, you need to be more careful. Those are expensive, over $5,000."

"I know, son, I'm sorry. I don't know what happened to them."

"Well, did you check the cup in the bathroom?"

"Yes, and I even checked the floor carefully."

"How about the bed table?"

"I even moved the table, checked the floor, and searched the bed while making it."

"Okay, Rachel and I are going to the supermarket later. We will stop and help you search. Damn, I hope we can find them because we don't want to have to buy new ones."

"Well, son, they are covered by insurance, are they not?"

"Dad, that's not the point. See you later."

"Thanks, son. Love you."

"Love you to, Dad."

Well, that didn't go too bad, and it didn't sound like he was too upset. I'm just a little upset about the $5,000!!

I will grab a beer and some snacks, sit in my easy chair, and watch football, Notre Dame and Michigan at 1:00 kickoff.

I must have dozed off again as I woke up with Brad turning down the TV volume. Standing beside him, Rachel smiled and said, "So Brad tells me you have lost your hearing aids."

"What?"

"I SAID, BRAD TELLS ME YOU HAVE LOST YOUR HEARING AIDS."

"Yeah, right. I have looked everywhere."

"WELL, YOU JUST SIT THERE AND WATCH YOUR BALL GAME, AND BRAD AND I WILL FIND THEM FOR YOU."

"Okay, thanks."

I watched them walking through the house and saw Rachel point at the stove, and they had a brief conversation. I wondered what that was all about. Rachel continued to search the kitchen and living room, looking under all the chairs and tables. Brad disappeared into the bedroom/bathroom. The Irish and Wolverines were tied 18 all going into the fourth quarter. They had been searching for almost an hour when Brad stepped out of the bedroom, signaling Rachel to follow him. About 10 minutes passed, and then they came into the TV room. Brad had my pill box in one hand and my hearing aids in the other. He handed me the hearing aids, and I quickly placed them in my ears.

Brad said, "Can you hear me, Dad?"

"Yes, I can hear you just fine. Where did you find them?"

"If you had taken your pills this morning *(oops, I didn't take my pills),* you would have found your hearing aids. They were in your pill box."

I could see it coming.

Brad continued, "Rachel and I will pick you up for church at 9:30 tomorrow, and we will go to the country club for brunch and have a family meeting."

Family meeting, this was serious.

"We have a lot to discuss. Not only did you lose your hearing aids, but you also didn't take your meds, you left your car door open in the garage, and Rachel found one of the gas burners was on for who knows how long."

I said, "I think since breakfast," and decided I probably shouldn't tell them about losing my cell phone.

"Okay, we need to go now. You enjoy your game. Love you, and we'll see you in the morning."

"Thanks, I love you guys, too."

After a few hugs and kisses from Rachel, they left just as Michigan kicked a field goal to win the game 28 to 25... bummer!! I had a TV dinner and watched the college football scoreboard show. It had been a hell of a day. It was now 7:30, so I took a shower, put on my pajamas, and jumped into bed, thinking I would turn on the TV and watch the 9:00 Stanford and Southern Cal game. Okay, dammit, where is the remote?

Well, maybe the retirement home won't be so bad. My friend Bob tells me there are a lot of lovely widow ladies there.

Dammit!

Bob lost his hearing aids and never found them. He thinks maybe he ate them because they looked like cashews. Dammit, it's hell to get old…

Job 12:12:
"So with old age is wisdom,
and with length of days understanding."

Dammit!

My girlfriend said, "I think it's time we take our relationship to the previous level... single."

Love

Dammit, I loved her... I am sitting here going through pictures from my college days. Her name was Debra, and if I hadn't been such an idiot, we would probably have married. I am sure it would have been a good marriage because she was a good, sensible, beautiful person, and I believe we loved each other. It was me; I blew it!!

Debbie and I met in college at a "freshman mixer." I spotted her across the room, a cute little blonde, and I approached and asked her to dance, which she accepted. She was an excellent dancer, following my moves with beauty and fluid grace. We continued to dance. She was laughing and smiling, as I was also. Song after song until the DJ played *New York, New York*, one of my favorites, and she commented that she also liked it. Soon, I noticed everyone had left the dance floor, leaving just the two of us. When we ended the dance with a graceful "dip," everyone applauded. That is when we shared our common interest in theater arts. With that began a whirlwind romance that lasted for three years.

We attended a small Christian college in central Ohio. Debbie was from just outside Cleveland, and I lived in Fort Wayne, Indiana, so we could keep the romance alive during summer break by spending weekends together. I worked in a paper processing plant that delivered paper products to printing companies. We worked 10-hour shifts Monday through Thursday and occasionally a few hours on Friday, but I could always head out shortly after noon to be in Cleveland before evening. Debbie worked for her parents in their insurance offices, so we could spend the weekends together until Sunday after the family lunch when I would head back to Fort Wayne. She visited me and my family in Fort Wayne several times. My family really liked her, especially my mother.

Debbie was very dedicated to her career. She majored in marketing with a minor in theater arts; she was a very talented singer and dancer. My major was theater arts, with a minor in communications. Our freshman and sophomore years were "storybook" times. The parties and the dances, with one of the highlights being our sophomore year when we both were granted the leads in the spring theater production of *West Side Story*. Six weeks and eight productions as Tony and Maria—almost unbelievable.

Our troubles began to occur in the second semester of our junior year. As I mentioned, Debbie was very dedicated to her education and career. She had accepted an apprenticeship at an advertising agency in Cleveland for the summer, hoping it would result in a full-time position when she graduated. As for me, I was still not concerned with my future, just the present, which included beer and parties. She kept pushing me to think about and start planning my future, resulting in heated discussions. All of this led to us agreeing to take the summer off and to see how we felt when we returned to school in the fall. We saw each other only twice that summer: once when I was invited to her older brother's wedding, and the other was when she visited Fort Wayne for my sister's 21st birthday celebration. I spent the summer working, playing baseball, and hanging out with friends. I did have a few dates, but nothing serious.

When we returned to school, she called me and suggested we get together and talk, which I was anxious to do. That meeting ended poorly, with another heated discussion about my lack of concern for the future. We did have a few dates after that meeting, but it did not feel the same as it had always felt. The "storybook" romance was no longer there.

In mid-October, I called her dorm room, and her roommate answered, telling me Debbie had gone home for the weekend. I questioned why she had not told me she was going home. Was there some family emergency, was someone ill? Her roommate seemed very uncomfortable with my question about why she had gone home. She did not know anything. It was strange because they had been roommates since they were first-year students and shared everything. I called and left messages for her several times after that, but she never returned them.

Several guys from Cleveland lived in my dorm, and one night at dinner, one of them asked if Debbie and I were still dating. When I asked why he had asked, he told me he was back in Cleveland and ran into her at the Oktoberfest party at the Country Club with her parents and some blond-headed dude. I immediately went to her dorm and sat in the lobby, waiting for her to return from her evening voice class. She looked surprised to see me, and I said we needed to talk. She said OKAY but wanted to take her backpack to her room and get a sweater, which she did, suggesting we take a walk.

On the walk across campus, when I asked about the "blond dude," she explained that he was a close friend. I ask her to define "close friend." They had met during the summer. He had graduated in the spring with an engineering degree and worked for a large corporation in Cleveland, which was paying him to get his master's degree from a local college. She admitted that she had feelings for him and still had feelings for me but was confused and needed time to sort things out. I believe I angrily commented, "Just what you have been looking for, a man with a future. Good luck with your future, but I don't want to play your game anymore."

I tried several times to call her and apologize, but she never returned the calls. When I saw her on campus, she avoided any contact or conversation. I finally accepted that it was over.

Then, after Christmas break, I learned she got engaged to a "blond dude" and was planning an August wedding. I called her and apologized, congratulated her on her engagement, and wished her the best in the future. She thanked me, wished me the best, and told me she would never forget our great times together, especially with Tony and Maria. Every once in a while, we would run into each other on campus and exchange cordial greetings.

We both graduated that spring, and she married the "blond dude" in August. I was told that after he completed his master's degree, the company transferred them to Denver. She was hired by what was considered the best advertising agency in Denver. She worked her way up in the company to senior vice president. With both of them dedicated to their careers, they never had any children.

I saw her one more time, ten years after we graduated, at a college homecoming. We were with a group of old friends having late-night drinks at the old "watering hole." I then learned that she and the "blond dude" divorced after eight years when she caught him with his secretary at a motel. So here we were, both divorced, talking about the old times when I brought up *West Side Story*, Maria and Tony. That's when she commented that I was still living the part of Tony. She said that I was stuck in time and had not moved forward. I was still the same guy, not thinking of the future, just yesterday and maybe today, but never tomorrow. The conversation deteriorated into a heated discussion. She finally just got up and walked away. I never saw her again but heard about her from mutual friends.

She never remarried; she just dedicated her time to her career. A very successful career, I might add.

Well, it's 35 years later, and here I am at 76 with two ex-wives, one grown child, two grandchildren, and an empty bank account.

After graduation, I took my dream job as manager and director of a theater in Louisville. Yep, I was getting to do it all, act and direct theater, but of course, you don't make any money doing theater. I married one of the actresses, April, and we had one child, a girl we named Autumn because she was born in the fall.

After three years together, April decided, much like Debbie, that I was worthless, going nowhere in life. She accepted an offer to go to Broadway and did quite well for herself. My daughter and granddaughter live in California, and I get to see them once a year. My second wife was also in the theater, a dancer, 15 years younger. That marriage only lasted three years until she ran off with another dancer.

Today, someone sent me an online obituary for Debbie, making me wonder, "What could have been?" I have heard it said that "women are crazy, but men are stupid." Well, I was stupid 56 years ago and then again ten years later. Dammit, Maria, I did love you!!

Dammit!

Proverb 31:26:
"She speaks with wisdom,
and faithful instruction is on her tongue."

Love Too

Damn, I loved him... I am sitting here going through pictures from my college days, waiting to die from liver cancer. The doctors have given me four to six months, and it has already been four months. I have accepted my fate, knowing that I am going to a better place. His name was Ron, and if he hadn't been such an idiot, we would probably have gotten married. I am sure it would have been a good marriage because he was good, sensible, and kind, and I believe we loved each other. It was probably my fault. I just wanted him to think about the future and where he was going!!

Ron and I met in college at a "freshman mixer." He was a cute guy with dark hair and a big smile. When he approached and asked me to dance, which I accepted, he was an excellent dancer, moving with fluid grace. I learned he was a theater major, explaining his dance talent; the theater was my minor. We continued to dance, laughing, smiling, and enjoying each other's company. Song after song, the DJ then announced an oldy but a goody and played *New York, New York*, one of my favorites, and he commented that he also liked it. Soon, I noticed that everyone, except the two of us, had left the dance floor. We weren't just dancing. It was like we were floating on air. It's a Fred Astaire and Ginger Rogers moment. A moment I will never forget. When we ended the dance with a graceful "dip," everyone applauded. With that began a whirlwind romance that lasted for three years.

We attended a small Christian college in central Ohio. Ron was from Fort Wayne, Indiana, and I lived just outside of

Cleveland, so we could keep the romance alive during summer break by spending weekends together. Ron worked at a paper processing plant that delivered paper products to printing companies. He worked 10-hour shifts Monday through Thursday and occasionally a few hours on Friday, but he could always head out shortly after noon to be in Cleveland before evening. I worked for my parents in their insurance offices so we could spend the weekends together until Sunday after the family lunch when he would head back to Fort Wayne. I visited him and his family in Fort Wayne several times. I liked his family.

I was very serious about my career, majoring in marketing with a minor in music and theater. I enjoyed singing and dancing. Ron's major was theater arts, with a minor in communications. Our first and second years were "storybook" times. The parties and the dances, with one of the highlights being our sophomore year when we both were granted the leads in the spring theater production of *West Side Story*. Six weeks and eight productions as Tony and Maria, it was almost unbelievable.

Our troubles began to occur in the second semester of our junior year. As I mentioned, I was very serious about my career. I wanted Ron to be more serious about his future or maybe our future, but he was only interested in the present. I had accepted an apprenticeship at an advertising agency in Cleveland for the summer. I hoped it would result in a full-time position when I graduated. As for Ron, he was still not concerned with the future, just the present, which included beer and parties. I kept pushing him to think about his future, resulting in heated discussions. All of this led to us agreeing to take the summer off and to see how we felt when we returned to school in the fall.

We saw each other only twice that summer, once when he was invited to my older brother's wedding. The other was when I visited Fort Wayne for his sister's 21st birthday celebration. I spent the summer working for the advertising agency. I did have a few casual dates, but nothing serious. Then I met Fred, a guy with his feet firmly planted on the ground and in control of his future. He had just graduated with a degree in engineering and worked with a huge corporation.

When we returned to school, Fred sent me very nice letters and called about once a week. Ron called me and suggested we get together and talk, which I was not anxious to do. I was confused about Ron and Fred, but I agreed to meet. The meeting did not go well, ending with another heated discussion about his lack of concern for the future.

We did have a few dates after that meeting, but it did not feel the same as it had always felt. The "storybook" romance was no longer there. In mid-October, I went home for the weekend and a date with Fred. We attended an Oktoberfest party at the Country Club with my parents.

When I had gone home for the weekend, Ron talked with my roommate, questioning why I had not told him that I was going home. He wanted to know if there was some family emergency. Was someone ill? My roommate said she was very uncomfortable and had told him she didn't know anything. Ron called and left messages several times when I returned, but I never responded to his calls. I was now even more confused about my relationships.

One of the guys in Ron's dorm told him he had seen me at the country club with Fred. Then when returning from an evening voice class, I was surprised to find Ron sitting in the dorm lobby waiting for me.

He said, "We need to talk."

I said okay and went to my room to drop off my backpack. I remember telling my roommate I didn't want to talk but could not continue to avoid him. I returned to the lobby, and we decided to take a walk.

On the walk across campus, when he asked about the "blond dude," I explained that he was a close friend. He asked me to explain "close friend." I explained that we had met during the summer. He had graduated in the spring with an engineering degree and worked for a large corporation in Cleveland that was paying him to get his master's degree from a local college. I admitted that I had feelings for Fred and that I also still had feelings for him, but I was confused and needed time to sort things out.

He angrily commented, "Just what you have been looking for, a man with a future. Good luck with your future, but I don't want to play your game anymore."

He tried several times to call and apologize, but I never returned the calls. We avoided contact or conversation when we saw each other on campus. I think we both finally accepted the fact that the "storybook" romance was over. Fred asked me to marry him during Christmas break, and I accepted. We set our plans for an August wedding after I graduated.

When we returned to campus, Ron learned that I was engaged. He called and apologized, congratulating me on the engagement and wishing me the best. I thanked him, telling him I would never forget our great times together, especially with Tony and Maria. Every once in a while, we would run into each other on campus and exchange cordial greetings.

We both graduated that spring, and I married Fred in August. After he completed his master's degree, the company transferred us to Denver. Fortunately, I got a job with the best advertising agency in Denver. I worked my way up in the company to senior vice president. Fred and I were both dedicated to our careers and never had children.

I saw Ron again at a college homecoming ten years after we graduated. We were with a group of old friends having late-night drinks at the old "watering hole." I learned he had divorced twice, and I had divorced after catching Fred with his secretary at a motel. Our marriage had lasted eight years.

Ron explained he was married twice with one grown child, two grandchildren, and an empty bank account. After graduation, he worked as manager and director of a theater in Louisville, where he still worked. He told me it was his dream job, acting and directing theater. His first wife was an actress named April, and they had one child, a girl they named Autumn because she was born in the fall.

He said, "After three years together, April decided, much like you, that I was worthless, going nowhere in life. She had accepted an offer to go to Broadway and did quite well for herself. My daughter and granddaughters live in California, and I see them maybe once a year."

Ron then told me that his second wife was also in the theater, a dancer, 15 years younger. That marriage only lasted three years until she ran off with another dancer.

So there we were, divorced, talking about the old times when he brought up *West Side Story*, Maria and Tony. That's when I made the stupid comment that he was still living the part of Tony, saying that he was stuck in time and had not moved forward. He seemed to be the same guy from college, not thinking of the future just yesterday and maybe today but never tomorrow. The conversation deteriorated into a heated discussion. I finally just got up and walked away. I never saw him again but heard about him from mutual friends and he had never married again. The last I heard about him, he was still with the Louisville Theater Company.

Today, someone sent me a clipping from the Louisville paper with a theater ad for *West Side Story*, directed by "Ronald Jenkins," which made me wonder, "What could have been?" I have heard it said that "women are crazy, but men are stupid." Well, I was crazy 56 years ago and then again ten years later. Dammit, Ron, I did love you!!

Thomas L. Rose

How is a man like the weather?
Nothing can be done to change either one of them.

Dammit!

*I gave the golf pro $20 to enter my scores in the computer handicap system. After the required 10 scores had been posted my handicap came back... **No Talent!!***

Goof

Dammit, I hate this game. In my group we call it "goof" because of the way we play. Let's put it this way, it's not the same game Tiger Woods plays! All of us in our foursome are in our 80's, so the goal is not to shoot par but our age.

So there we were on the 17th tee, a par three that plays 155 yards from the senior tee. I'm 83 and with two holes to play my total is 75, meaning all I needed to do to shoot my age was to play the last two holes in 8 shots. With this par three and the par four 18th I need one par and one bogey. I stood on the tee, looking at the flag, trying to decide what club to use. The pin is located on the left at the back of the green so I decided to hit my 7 wood to the center of the green to avoid the large sand trap that borders the left side of the green. I usually hit a fade *(ball moves from left to right)* so I aimed slightly left to curve the ball to the center of the green. I made a good swing hitting the ball in the center of the club, meaning the ball was not going to curve right and I had aimed left. That is when Charlie, my friend and golfing partner, called out "beach party" as my ball landed on the left side of the green... and with two hops settled in the middle of the sand trap. Damn!!

"Nice swing but tough break, partner," commented Charlie as he stepped to the tee. As the two older guys (we're both 83) Charlie and I are always partners playing Mike and George, the young guys (aged 80 and 82). Charlie hit a good shot but was just barely on the front of the green with a very long and difficult birdie putt and not a sure par. Mike and George had hit their shots just short of the green. By the way, the match was dead even at this point. The losers buy the beer and hot dogs, so we were talking some "big" money.

The four of us have been friends for many years. In fact, Charlie, George and I went to school here and have lived here all our lives. After retiring from the military, Mike moved here with his wife Marge, who died 3 years ago from breast cancer. Our wives have also been good friends as long as we have. When we play golf they always go to lunch and shopping. We always joke that what we lose playing golf is not close to what we may be losing with their shopping!!

We drove up to the green and walked to our individual shots. Charlie was the only one who was on the green. Of course, I was in the sand trap. Mike and George were short of the green by about 10 yards and as we say in golf, "out" means "farthest from the pin," so they were first to hit their shots.

Mike hit first and left the ball about 5 feet below the hole. Seeing Mike's shot come up short, George hit his about 3 feet above the hole, leaving him a very difficult fast downhill putt. I then set up for my sand shot. My plan was to slide the club under the ball, loft it in the air, land it softly on the green about halfway to the hole, and have it "run out" to the hole. Well sometimes things don't work out as planned, especially in golf. The club did not exactly slide under the ball, more like hit it in the center, or as we say the "gut," barely cleared the edge of the trap and scooted rapidly to the far side of the green. Charlie, not wanting to be above the hole, left the ball about 4 feet below the hole just past where Mike's ball rested.

It was now my turn from about 30 feet away and slightly uphill. I struck a pretty good putt which ended up about a foot past the hole.

Mike said, "That's good," and knocked the ball back to me.

Bogie four, so I now needed to par the last hole to shoot my age.

Then it was time for Mike to putt straight up the hill from about 5 feet on the same line as Charlie's putt from about 4 feet so he should have gotten a good idea how his putt would roll. The putt just slid by on the left side by a couple of inches.

Commenting, "Tough break," I picked up his ball and handed it to him.

It was Charlie's turn to putt. He asked me what I thought, and we agreed that the putt was going to break left and he needed to hit it firm just outside of the hole on the right. Good old Charlie struck the putt firmly, and it dropped in the center of the hole. I gave him a big pat on the back.

Now it was time for George's tricky downhill putt to keep the match tied. He and Mike conferred on the line and speed and then the "old fart" stepped up, barely tapped the ball, and it very slowly rolled down the hill and slipped into the right side of the hole. The match remained even going to the 18th hole.

This group originally totaled eight, two foursomes, but we are now down to just four. Two have gone to that big course in the sky. One by heart attack and the other died from cancer. Number three is living in a retirement home with his wife, but he suffers from dementia. We all visit him occasionally, but he hardly remembers us. And the other, after the death of his wife, moved to Florida to live with his son and family. We keep in touch by email, and last year my wife and I were able to take time to visit him during our trip to Florida. He and I were even able to get in a round of golf.

The remaining four of us golf 2 to 3 times a week during golf season, and in the winter months we play cards two days a week, cribbage one day and poker the other.

Occasionally the wives will talk us into playing euchre, but we will not play bridge, no bridge!!

Charlie is my oldest friend. He owned the hardware store next to my insurance office, and his wife Ellen is probably my wife's best friend. They both worked as tellers at the First National Bank until my wife joined me in the insurance office when I purchased it from the previous owner. Charlie and I retired about the same time when I sold the agency to a young agent who had been working for me. Charlie's son and son-in-law took over his hardware store.

George was the town barber and worked by himself for many years, but as the town grew he added chairs, three in total, and sold the shop to the other three barbers a short time after Charlie and I retired.

Mike is the "new guy" who along with his wife and son moved to town about 40 years ago after retiring from the Marines and opened a bicycle shop which his daughter and son-in law are now operating with Mike's "close supervision." He was an officer in the U.S. Army Delta Force which he doesn't talk about much, but sometimes after a few beers he will share a story. Mike's wife died from breast cancer 6 years ago, and it became the mission of the other wives to find him someone with whom he could share his life. About a year ago they succeeded in matching him up with Anne, a pretty English woman whose charming accent seems to have "disarmed" the Delta Force Sergeant. In fact, after our last round of golf he told us they were talking about moving in together. He said he was struggling with how to tell his kids. We assured him that they all loved Annie and would be happy for them.

So there we stood on the 18th tee, par four, 318 yards from the forward tee, slight dogleg right, with pond fronting the green. The match was all even and I needed a par to shoot my age. We still had the honor, and I told Charlie to step and lead us to victory. He hit a perfect drive with just a little movement right into the dogleg. I stepped up and hit my drive right next to Charlie's so we were both in good shape for our approach shots to the green.

George hit a nice drive in the fairway but not quite as long as my golf partner and I. Mike, the long hitter in the group, lined up his drive to cut the corner and shorten the hole which he usually does. He took his mighty swing and the ball headed down the right side but it was drifting a little too far right and hit the big oak tree at the corner of the fairway. We heard it hit the tree and were sure he was in the woods, but it kicked out to the center of the fairway about 10 to 15 yards in front of all of us. As we headed down the fairway my golf partner and I were doing a little "trash talk," calling him a "lucky ass."

George was the first to hit his second shot and we heard him yell, "Go, go, go!!" Well, it went right in the center of the pond in front of the green.

After a few expletives Charlie said to Mike, "Sorry, partner, it's now in your hands."

Mike said, "No problem, partner, I've got it covered."

Charlie hit his shot next with the same result as George, landing at the bottom of the pond. He said nothing, just looked at me and slammed his club in the bag.

Now it was me against Mike, one-on-one. I stepped up and hit my shot, one of my best of the day, on the green about 30 feet below the hill. I looked over at Mike and said, "Beat that lucky."

Mike mumbled something about me not being that good. He then selected his club, stepped up to his ball, hesitated, and asked his partner about the distance. They conferred for a few seconds and then he changed his club selection. After a little heckling from Charlie he hit his shot. It was a great looking shot but just a little long over the back of the green. He quickly commented, "Damn, I was thinking I needed more club, should have stayed with my original choice."

Charlie was quick to comment, "I've told you before, Mike, you don't have the right equipment for that thinking." After a "one finger" salute from Mike we proceeded to the green.

Charlie and George both hit their penalty shots onto the green, two in, three out, four on. They both hit really good shots within a foot or so of the hole, gimmes, and I flipped the balls back to them.

Now it was between Mike and me to decide the match. I had the advantage with a straight uphill putt from about 30 feet, and Mike had a very difficult downhill chip shot from over the back of the green which he knocked about 25 feet past the hole just in front of where my ball rested. So I had a 30-foot birdie to win the match and shoot one under my age. The putt was almost straight up the hill with maybe a little movement to the left but not much. The important thing was to get the ball to the hole.

I was careful, telling myself, "Get the ball to the hole." Well, I got the ball to the hole okay but about 3 feet past the hole, leaving myself a tough little quick downhill putt. That was not the worst thing because if Mike didn't make this putt then I would still have my putt to win the match.

Mike stepped up and hit the ball firmly. We all watched it climb up the hill, and I was thinking this was going to be further past the hole than my ball. The ball hit the edge of the hole, made a 360-degree turn around the hole, and dropped to the bottom for a par. Now I needed to make my putt to tie the match and shoot my age.

Charlie and I both took a good look at the line and decided it was just outside the hole on the left. It was going to be quick and move right. I just barely tapped the ball and it rolled slowly down the hill, caught the right side of the hole, and like Mike's, made a 360-degree turn around the hole… but unlike Mike's, my ball ended up finishing about 6 inches below the hole.

So I shot one over my age. Charlie and I lost the match, and we would be buying the hot dogs and beer. As we headed to the parking lot Mike and George were doing a little "nettling" but it was all in good fun. Maybe next time it will be our turn to "stick in the needle." Dammit, sometimes I may hate the game, but I do love these guys…

I came home from my annual physical exam, changed my clothes, grabbed my golf clubs and as I was headed out the door my wife questioned, "Where are you going?"

I explained that the doctor said, "You need more greens."

Dammit!

"Once we arrive in the cemetery, we are equal."
- Thomas L. Rose

The Cemetery

Dammit, maybe we weren't crazy old folks. There is a cemetery that borders my neighborhood where all of us "old folks" take our daily walk. It is a beautiful place to walk with all the great trees and the beautiful flowers families have left at the grave sites. It is especially nice with the smell of fresh cut grass just after the cemetery crew has mowed. All throughout the year we try to walk every morning around 8:30, sometimes slow or fast depending on the weather. But when it is nice we walk along sharing the latest gossip and our medical conditions. For example, someone might say, "You know, my arthritis was really bad yesterday," or "I need to call the doctor about my backache." And we are always afraid that if we are not with the group then they will be talking about us.

We all remember the grave sites by the names on the stones, like "the Johnson family plots are just past the big oak tree," and "the Millers, Sarah and William, are buried just past the water faucet." We can remember all of this information, but sometimes we can't remember what we did yesterday or what day it is.

As I said, the cemetery can be very beautiful, but it can also be kind of scary with some of the grave sites having those solar charged lights, especially if there is a little fog. Even during the day it can be mysterious. There are several graves of murder victims, one of a fallen police officer, as well as several World War I, World War II, and Civil War soldiers.

There is one grave in particular that triggers our imagination, which has a large stone with the inscription:

"Willy Wilson, 1890 to 1942." We have all found it strange that there is no grass growing on Willy's grave. It's just like someone has intentionally killed the grass around the grave. Also there always seemed to be a lot of dead flowers lying around the site. Sometimes the dirt looks fresh like it is a new grave or maybe the cemetery crew has planted grass, but it never seems to grow. Several times we have thought it looked like the stone had been moved a little in one direction or the other or at least turned slightly. How could that be?? Perhaps it is just the imagination of "crazy old people" with bad memories!!

Well one day we noticed what looked like a black rose on top of Willy's stone or maybe it was a dead red rose, but it was definitely a rose, and we began to let our imaginations run wild with all kinds of explanations. By the time we got back to the neighborhood we had a full blown legend created. That is when I decided to do some research, as my son always told me you can find anything on the Internet, so I began my search. I started with "Willy Wilson" and came up with 277 results for Willy Wilson in the state. Then I tried "Willy Wilson 1860" but came up with nothing. So then I tried "Willy Wilson 1942." Bingo!! There it was, an article from August 17, 1942, in the *Daily Gazette*:

Suspect Arrested in Martin Murder

Wilson (Willy) Wilson arrested and charged with the murder of high school teacher, Mary Louise Martin. She was found dead in her home August 9th. Cause of death as confirmed by coroner Dr. Ben Hoover and announced by Sheriff Otis Miller on August 12th was strangulation. Wilson is also an employee of the high school as math teacher and the head football coach.

The sheriff's report alleges that the murder was the result of a "lovers quarrel." Sheriff Miller reported that the arrest of Wilson was the result of information he received from the deceased's brother, Charlie Jones. The brother told the sheriff his sister was involved with a secret lover, a married man, and that he was not sure of his identity but thought maybe it was Wilson. Mr. Wilson and his wife, Mary Anne, had been separated for over a year and she had moved back to her hometown and had proceeded to file for a divorce.

When the sheriff arrived to question Wilson he appeared to be in a highly agitated state of mind. As the sheriff described, "Mr. Wilson was screaming like a maniac about how he hated women, that they were evil and should die." Deputies had to restrain Wilson and he was taken to the county jail, was booked and placed in a cell where he continued his uncontrollable rant about women. Unable to reason with Wilson, the sheriff transferred him to the General Hospital mental ward where he is being held under guard by deputies.

I continued my Internet search and learned that after several weeks of treatment by doctors at the hospital, Wilson was returned to the county jail and was charged with the murder of Mary Louise Martin.

I then did a Google search on the victim, Mary Louise Martin, and again was successful and found an article from August 12th, 1942, in the *Daily Gazette*:

Local School Teacher Strangled

High school teacher, Mary Louise Martin, age 42 was found dead in her home August 11ᵗʰ. Her apparent cause of death was strangulation according to Sheriff Otis Miller, but Dr. Ben Hoover, the county coroner, will be performing an autopsy and filing a report in the next few days.

Mrs. Martin had been teaching English and Music at the high school for the last ten years and was well known for her beautiful singing voice as leader of the Methodist church choir. She was a widow, having lost her husband Gordon in a railroad accident in 1939. She was the mother of two children, United States Air Force Lieutenant George Martin, Pamela (Martin) Williams of San Francisco, California, and granddaughter Amanda Williams, age two. Her parents, Gerald and Hilda Jones preceded her in death. Her father Gerald had owned Jones' Hardware Store, which is now owned and operated by her brother Charlie Jones. Mrs. Martin lived at 602 Mayflower Drive. Neighbors were shocked by her murder and commented that she was very friendly, always happy and smiling.

Funeral arrangements are pending the autopsy. The sheriff reports that at this time there are no suspects but assures residents the full force of the sheriff's department will be working to solve this murder quickly.

Look for more in the Daily Gazette next week...

I also found another article dated September 7th, 1942, from the *Weekly Gazette*:

Accused Murderer to Appear in Court

Wilson (Willy) Wilson charged with the murder of high school teacher, Mary Louise Martin, appeared in court today. Miss Martin was found dead in her home August 9th. After a brief investigation by the sheriff's department, Wilson was arrested and charged with first degree murder. Having refused legal counsel and asking to represent himself for the proceedings, Mr. Wilson pleaded guilty to the murder in front of Criminal Court Judge Owen Kramer. Judge Kramer suggested the defendant reconsider having a defense lawyer. Wilson confirmed that he wanted to represent himself and pleaded guilty to the charge of murder.

After his arrest for the murder of Martin, Wilson spent several weeks under the psychological care of doctors at General Hospital. After the plea by Wilson, Judge Kramer asked District Attorney Walter Cannon if doctors had cleared Wilson to be mentally stable to make rational decisions about this own life. Cannon assured the judge that the doctors had released Wilson with the assurance of reading a statement of confirmation from the hospital.

Judge Kramer then asked Wilson if he wanted to change his plea, but Wilson confirmed that he wanted to represent himself and pleaded guilty to the charge of murder. The judge then said he would accept the guilty plea but would not pronounce sentence until he completed a review of the case.

Sheriff Miller explained to reporters that apparently Mrs. Martin was ending their relationship and that this along with the divorce papers from Wilson's wife pushed Wilson over the edge. He became enraged and strangled Martin. Wilson also admitted to the authorities that he had planned on killing his wife. Fortunately for his wife, Wilson was arrested before he could reach her. The judge will pronounce sentence for Wilson on September 15th.

Further Internet research revealed that after one more time affirming that Wilson still wanted to continue as his own legal representative, Judge Owen Kramer sentenced Wilson (Willy) Wilson to death by electrocution for the first degree murder of Mary Louise Martin. Wilson was remanded to the State Prison to await execution, which was administered on October 31st, 1942. The *Daily Gazette* reporting from November 1st, 1942, was as follows:

Convicted Murderer Executed on Halloween

Wilson (Willy) Wilson was convicted for the murder of school teacher Mary Louise Martin, on September 7th 1942. Judge Owen Kramer had sentenced him to death by electrocution at the state prison where he had been incarcerated for the last 2 months. Wilson had rejected all opportunities to appear before the court of appeals to have his sentence reduced. He said he wanted to die so he could come back and strangle all women including his ex-wife. It was reported by execution witnesses that even his last words reflected his hatred of women. The warden reported that during his stay at the state prison he had written many letters to the media expressing his hatred of women but fortunately none had ever been published. Wilson had requested that he be executed on Halloween which seems appropriate to this reporter for such a mad man.

It was a beautiful fall day, temperature in the high fifties, and the leaves had all turned to their rainbow of fall colors as our group walked through the cemetery. When we reached Willy Wilson's grave site, I took the opportunity to share my research with the group and they were all fascinated, asking a lot of questions that I could not answer.

One of the group, a retired doctor, explained to the group saying, "Sometimes at an execution the prisoner's eyeballs sometimes pop out and that the prisoner often defecates, urinates, and vomits blood. That the body turns bright red as its temperature rises, and the prisoner's flesh swells and his skin stretches to the point of breaking. Sometimes the prisoner catches fire and witnesses hear sounds like bacon frying, and the sickly smell of burning flesh fills the chamber." Several of the ladies almost fainted and I will admit I experienced a few "quakes" in my stomach.

November 1st, 2020, our friend Carl, who lives close to the cemetery entrance, called all of us and reported significant police activity in the cemetery. Since it was a cold and rainy day the group would not be walking so Carl and I, with raincoats on and umbrellas in hand, decided to check it out.

The police had the area completely roped off so the best we could see were police around a newer model black Buick SUV which looked to be in front of Willy's grave site. A news reporter told us that he understood that a woman had been found dead in that car but that was all he knew.

So we wandered back to Carl's place and shared coffee with several of our group where Carl reported that he had seen a black Buick enter the cemetery on several occasions. Could that be the same Buick he and I had observed today? We were all glued to the TV awaiting any news breaks but none came all day.

Then during the 6:00 pm news the police chief had a press conference announcing that a woman had been found dead in her car at the cemetery and that the cause of death was undetermined. Her name was being withheld until the family had been contacted, promising he would have more on the late news at 11:00. The news station showed a few pictures of the murder site and it appeared the car was parked in front of Willy's grave site. Very interesting...

Like myself, I would guess that our whole group stayed up a couple of hours longer waiting for additional information on the murder. The murder was the lead story on the 11:00 news with a live press conference by the police chief.

He explained, "At 6:47 AM today the department dispatcher received a phone call from the sexton at the Community Cemetery who reported that as he was making his daily rounds of the cemetery, he had come across a black Buick in which there was a woman. The car was locked and she did not respond when he pounded on the windows. Officers arrived at 6:58 AM and accessed the car to find the woman was dead. The officers secured the area and contacted the crime lab who arrived a short time later and determined that the woman had died from apparent strangulation. The coroner later confirmed that the cause of death was by strangulation and that she had died somewhere between the hours of 11:00 PM and 1:00 AM. Mrs. Amanda Williams Jenkins, aged 83, lived in the family home at 602 Mayflower Drive. Her family, who reside in California, have been notified and will be making funeral arrangements with details to follow in the next few days. At this time we have no suspects in the murder of Mrs. Jenkins. We are waiting to talk with family when they arrive to see if they can supply any information on who might have wanted to harm her. We would also appreciate any information from friends and associates of Mrs. Jenkins. If anyone saw or knows anything about this crime, please call the police hotline at 566-6666."

The chief then answered several "stupid" questions from reporters.

At almost midnight, two hours past my usual bedtime, I turned off the lights and TV. It didn't take long for sleep to come. My dreams were about the murder and questions began to come to me. Wasn't Mary Martin's granddaughter's name Amanda Williams? Didn't Mary Martin live on Mayflower Drive?

I awoke suddenly at 5:00 AM with all of these questions racing around in my head. I made a cup of coffee and sat down at the computer to answer my questions and quickly confirmed that Amanda Jenkins was Mary Martin's granddaughter living in her grandmother's home at 602 Mayflower Drive. Further research revealed that after retiring from her job as a mental health nurse and the death of her husband, Amanda Williams had moved from California to her grandmother's home. I called a friend who lived on Mayflower Drive, and he said that he did know her but that she was very strange and kept to herself. The kids in the neighborhood all called her the "crazy" lady.

I called Carl and told him what I had learned, and he said that we needed to discuss this with the others and that he would contact them. It was another cold rainy day, so he suggested that we meet at his house for coffee.

When I arrived everyone was there anxiously waiting to hear my information about Mrs. Amanda Williams. I told everyone what I had learned and then Carl suggested we review the following facts:

#1 Willy Wilson had murdered, strangled Mrs. William's grandmother.

#2 Mrs. Williams was found dead, strangled in front of Willy Wilson's grave.

#3 Someone had killed all the grass on Willy's grave and left dead flowers.

#4 Mrs. Williams' neighbors thought she was strange, and the kids called her crazy.

#5 We had all thought that Willy's stone had been moved several times.

#6 Willy's wishes were to be executed on Halloween so he could come back and kill women.

We all then speculated that Mrs. Williams had been the person who killed the grass on Willy's grave and left the dead flowers... and she was crazy!! Had Willy somehow managed one more female victim? Should we tell the police our theory? No, they would just think we were crazy old people with wild imaginations!!

One year later, Halloween 2021, it was a beautiful fall day, and we were on our regular walk and stopped in front of Willy Wilson's grave which was now covered with green grass and the stone had been set square. The case of Mrs. Amanda Martin Williams still remained unsolved.

Dammit, maybe we should have told the police our theory? Well, they couldn't arrest Willy anyhow because he was dead.

*"Cemeteries contain many mysteries.
Most never to be solved."*

- Unknown

Dammit!

*"I have heard it said that the older you get, the better you get.
That may be true if you are a bottle of wine
but not if you are a banana."*

- Thomas L. Rose

Old Geezer

Dammit, we're over 80 so they call us "old geezers." So, I decided to look up the meaning of "geezer" on the computer. Yes, an old geezer can use a computer!!

"Geezer" is an informal and sometimes mildly disparaging slang term for an old man. It can also refer to someone eccentric, unreasonable, or set in their ways.

In the United Kingdom, "geezer" can also be used to refer to any man, regardless of age, and can be used in a complimentary way. For example, you might say, "He is a good geezer."

However, we are not in the United Kingdom, so why don't you young "whipper snappers" knock off the "old geezer" crap. Please address us with the respect we deserve: Mister, Sir or maybe our name will do. I once saw a restaurant sign that referred to those over 80 as "recycled teenagers."

Please understand the following:

We were born in the 1940's and grew up in the 1940's and 1950's. Our education occurred in the 1950's and 1960's from apolitical teachers, concentrating on education rather than political views. School discipline was supported by parents and some teachers were feared but all were respected. We dated in the 1950's and 1960's and many of us married in the 1960's and started our families.

We have lived through eight decades (*some of us nine*) and two different centuries. We heard the famous lines by Winston Churchill in 1941, "*Never, never give up,*" and in 1987 by Ronald Reagan, "*Tear down this wall.*" And along with our fellow Americans we experienced the launch of the first mission to the moon on July 16, 1969, and the horrors of September 11, 2001.

We progressed from party line telephones, using an operator to make long distance calls, to today when we can make a video call anywhere around the world on our "smartphone." We have gone from handwritten letters and penny postcards to emails on our computers and text messages on our cell phones. Yes, we learned to use computers with punch cards, and floppy disks, and now we have the "cloud." We know about gigabytes and megabytes; we can't explain them, but we know they exist because they are on our cell phones.

Most of us didn't have televisions in our homes until the mid-1950's. We listened to the radio, including shows like *The Green Hornet*, *Roy Rogers*, *Sky King*, and *Buster Brown* (*Hi, my name is Buster Brown I live in a shoe, that's my dog Tag he lives there too*). Then along came black & white TV and soon after color. Our parents made sure we stayed at least three feet back from the screen.

As for music, we grew up with Louis Armstrong, Frank Sinatra, Peggy Lee, Ella Fitzgerald, and all the greats of the Big Band and Jazz era. We were there for the birth of rock 'n' roll and when Ed Sullivan introduced Elvis and later The Beatles. We danced to *Rock Around the Clock, Blue Berry Hill* and went to all of the "Gidget" and "Elvis" movies. We watched Dick Clark and *American Bandstand*. There were "sock hops" with Be Bop, and The Stroll, all leading to the

Monkey and the Twist. We wore pegged pants, penny loafers, letter jackets, and senior cords, and dated girls in poodle skirts and bobby socks. We let them wear our letter sweaters and jackets, and we exchanged class rings to "go steady."

We lived through polio, infantile paralysis, tuberculosis, ringworm, swine flu, and most recently COVID-19. We rode tricycles, bicycles, roller skates, scooters, and mopeds all without helmets. We drove cars with a "straight stick" and now we have automatic transmissions, backup cameras, and GPS on our hybrids and some automobiles even drive themselves. Soon we will travel like they do on *Star Trek... beam me up, Scotty!*

Oh yes, we were also the "pranksters" who on Halloween placed the "cow pie" (dung) in a paper sack, lit it on fire on a front porch, and rang the doorbell then waited for the resident to open the door and "stomped it out." The other favorite was to "stick a car horn." That's right, back then the horn was not connected to the ignition switch so you could honk it without the key. Sticking a toothpick along the side of the horn button would do the job. Leaving your car unlocked in your driveway was an invitation to having a stuck horn. We were also the ones who placed the outhouse on the front steps of the high school.

Most of our memories are good, except that many of us were sent to war in Vietnam and when we came home, unlike our fathers from World War II and Korea, there were no ticker tape parades. We were not welcomed home as heroes but as outcasts. Shame on those who made these brave men feel as though they were criminals.

At a dinner party recently a young person (age 50) asked several of us over 80 what we had learned that we would like to share with the younger generations. Well, jokingly, we all answered, "How much time do you have??" Without giving it a whole lot of thought we came up with the following:

- *"I have learned that family and friends are the most important things in life. Without them I would never have made it into my 80's. They helped guide me through the dark days of my life."*

- *"I avoid people who don't value me or my time. They might not know my worth, but I do."*

- *"I have learned to give compliments freely and when I receive a compliment, I never turn it down, I just say thank you."*

- *"I have learned not to be embarrassed by my emotions; they are part of being human. I shed tears at the loss of loved ones and feel and cherish the memories."*

- *"I have learned to say 'love' to friends and family as often as I can. Also to love myself because if you don't love yourself, it is very difficult to love others and to have others love me."*

- *"I am doing what makes me happy. I have learned that happiness is a choice, so you just need to choose to be happy. Even when I am unhappy, I'm happy that I can be unhappy."*

- *"I have learned that positive thoughts lead to a positive attitude and that being positive makes me feel much better than a negative attitude. My glass is always half full."*

- *"I take each day for whatever it gives me. I have learned to live each day as if it is my last, and one day it will be my last, however I will go having lived a great life."*

- *"Living life is like writing a book, we get to write all the chapters except the last one which He gets to write."*

- *"I have learned that God is there for you when you need him. He has always been there, I just didn't always go to Him when I should have."*

- *"I remember when I thought I knew everything. But now I know I don't know anything."*

In this "old geezer's" opinion one of the failures of our civilization is the failure to learn from our past. The failure to listen to our older generations. To learn from their mistakes. To ask them to share their experience and knowledge to improve their own and future generations. Our educational system fails to take advantage of the experience and knowledge of us "old geezers." We are here waiting to share if we are just asked.

So dammit, before you call someone an "old geezer," remember where he has been and what he has seen. Maybe you could learn something if you listened to him.

Dammit!

.

"The young man thinks he knows the rules,
but the old man knows the rules and the exceptions.
The young man should learn from the old man."

- Oliver Wendell Holmes Sr.

"He who has health, has hope;
and he who has hope, has everything."

- Thomas Carlyle

Dammit!

*"I didn't need to look for Waldo.
I always knew where he was."*

- Thomas L. Rose

Waldo, the Writer

Dammit, he was a good friend; I saw in the paper that he passed away on May 14th. This was a significant date for Waldo, which I will explain later. Who was Waldo? He looked similar to Waldo, which we have all tried to find in the puzzle picture, but not the same guy. My Waldo was Walter Bibbler, better known to all his friends by his high school nickname, Waldo. He was tapped for his nickname when the freshman English teacher read his name for attendance as Waldo Bibbler (a class list typo), and the name stuck through high school and beyond. He graduated from high school in 1958 with the rest of the Sahib club, not a gang but a club with a clubhouse above a friend's garage that we decorated with stolen street signs. But the Sahib club is a story for a later time.

Waldo was always loose and happy even though he was from a broken home and had no idea if his father was dead or alive or where he lived. An alcoholic who ran off when Waldo was very young, leaving his mother to raise him alone, and she did an excellent job; every one of the guys loved Waldo's mom, especially for her double chocolate chip cookies.

Although it was the 1950s, the music was the beginning of rock 'n' roll with Chubby Checker and, of course, Elvis. But even though we loved our music, Waldo taught his friends to appreciate jazz. As I remember, his jazz album collection was over 100 with greats like Louis Armstrong, Artie Shaw, Lionel Hampton, Stan Kenton, and his very favorite, Duke Ellington. We would have been at his concert if Ellington was in the area. Waldo even organized a trip to the Newport Jazz Festival in

1957. There we were, six guys in a 1954 Chevy, camping gear on the roof, and very little money in our pockets. When we arrived home, between the six of us we had exactly one dollar and 62 cents. To five of us, the 5 days were a great experience, but to Waldo, it was the ultimate experience. He also introduced us to great vocalists like Frank Sinatra and Ella Fitzgerald. Yes, Waldo should have been born in 1930, not 1940.

I was Waldo's first grade classmate in parochial school and then we continued through to the public high schools. His somewhat quiet, dry sense of humor was always with him. When he talked, you had to pay close attention or else you could miss a "gem." This was always a challenge for the nuns in parochial school. They all loved Waldo, or Walter at that time, but they could not figure him out.

He was the one who challenged Sister Mary Catherine when she strongly suggested the boys should not have long hair by suggesting Jesus had long hair, to which she responded that when he could walk on water, he could have long hair. I believe he got even with her in what we all called the "cooperation incident." Sister had decided when we were in the 8th grade that we should begin to learn some of the "social graces" like dancing. Once a week, we would go to the big music room on the second floor where Sister would teach us dancing, such as the Foxtrot, the Waltz, and others. One of these lessons was square dancing, which Waldo hated. So, on that particular occasion, he snuck out of the room and hid on the fire escape. Well, of course, Sister caught him, and as punishment, he was to write a paper on cooperation. The next day, Waldo showed up with a two-page paper on cooperation. Unfortunately, before looking at the paper, she asked him to read it to the class. So Waldo read his cooperation masterpiece on The Farm Bureau Co-op to the chuckles of all his classmates.

Waldo's mischief-making adventures continued through high school when the trigonometry teacher, Mr. Cooper, completed a complicated equation on the blackboard and asked the class if there were any questions. Waldo said yes and asked, "Should chicken be eaten with the fingers, or should the fingers be eaten separately?" Again, there was a classroom full of chuckles.

As you can see by now, Waldo was very creative. Our senior year it was his idea to go out into the country and steal an outhouse, bring it back, and place it on the school front steps, which we accomplished. Of course, we were caught, but Waldo tried to explain to the principal that it was to be part of his final submission for art class (he was also a good artist). He explained that it would be used in a giant sculpture he intended to donate to the school. That sounded good to me, but it didn't fly with the principal, and we had to return the outhouse to its home.

But his greatest comic escapades probably occurred in Senior English, where our teacher, Miss Good, who had been teaching English from the beginning of time, loved to assign the writing of these papers by giving us a subject or words to use. No matter the subject or words, Waldo's stories always occurred at the Red Dog Saloon. For example, if the subject was snow, his story would be "The Day It Snowed at the Red Dog Saloon," or if it was love, of course, it was "The Day Love Almost Destroyed the Red Dog Saloon." Waldo was never a great believer in love. However, later in his life, he fell in love and married a great gal.

May 14th was a significant day in Waldo's life because it was the day in 1958, just before our graduation, when there was a ceremony at the school where they announced all of the class awards and college scholarships. Before I proceed with the events of that day, I need to explain what happened before the event.

As I explained, Waldo always wrote his senior English papers about the Red Dog Saloon. Miss Good did not appreciate his sense of humor. She never stopped him from writing about the Red Dog Saloon, saying she respected everyone's right to free expression. I sincerely believe she enjoyed his stories and looked forward to the next chapter, as did the class. However, most of the time, Waldo received "C" grades on his class assignments. Waldo discovered that his mother's garage door opener also opened Miss Good's garage door. Not a good thing for Miss Good, whose garage door would magically go up late at night!

You should also be aware that Waldo wrote a gossip column for the school newspaper, usually involving students; you know who was dating who... and who broke up with who. Sometimes, it concerned teachers, which was not to their liking. Waldo never used real names, so it was hard for a teacher to call him out. As the saying goes, they just had to "grin and bear it."

Understanding that his mother was not going to be able to pay for his college education, Waldo had worked some part-time jobs and saved a little money, but certainly not enough for him to attend a college or university except maybe the local college where he could work and live at home, which was his plan. However, several friends suggested he apply for some available scholarships. In particular, we all thought he should take his Red Dog Saloon papers and create a short story for the

Literary Society Scholarship. After much prodding, he agreed and submitted his story and application.

Back to May 14th, 1958, senior awards day. After the senior awards were announced, the scholarships were awarded. Each of these announcements were made by the school department heads, so Miss Good was to announce the English scholarships. These were given to her in sealed envelopes, which she opened and read the names. She had announced several smaller scholarships when she came to the two biggies, The Journalism and Literary Society scholarships. She opened the Journalism scholarship, sponsored by the county newspapers, smiled, and read the name Walter T. Bibbler; I forgot to tell you he had also applied for that scholarship. Then came the time for the largest of the English department scholarships, The Literary Society scholarship, funded generously by several of the more affluent families in the community. Again, Miss Good opened the envelope, paused what seemed like an eternity and finally read the name Walter T. Bibbler. The whole auditorium stood and applauded. I still wonder what Miss Good thought when the student she had given "C" grades to was just awarded two of the largest scholarships available. I bet she would never admit it, but she felt good, as we all did. I was so happy because, with these two scholarships, my friend Waldo could attend the university of his choice.

Waldo attended a Big Ten university, graduated at the top of his class, finished grad school, and eventually became head of the English Department. We kept up through the years with letters, class reunions, and, of course, emails in later years. In his last email about a month ago, he explained he had been diagnosed with liver cancer and was told he had about eight months to live, but he only made it three. May he rest in peace.

My friend, who only received "C" grades in Senior English, became the head of a university English department. While I, who received "A" and "B" grades in English, sit here struggling to write this short story. Dammit, where did I go wrong!!

"Success is going from failure to failure without loss of enthusiasm."

- Winston Churchill

Authors Note

It only seems fitting that since several of these stories were written during the COVID pandemic that I include these stories and comments about a terrible time in my life as I am sure it was for others.

Dammit!

"During COVID they told us to avoid touching our face.
My solution to avoid that was to have
a glass of wine in each hand."

- Thomas L. Rose

Pandemic

Dammit, the COVID pandemic changed our lives forever, most of it wrong. The deaths from COVID weren't bad enough, but suicides, divorces, and business failures all increased significantly. The fear and uncertainty that it created for some was unbearable. I lost a good friend and neighbor to suicide. He had lost his wife a few months before the pandemic "lock down" and he was lonely and depressed. We talked on the phone daily, but he could not be without his loving wife. Being unable to go out and be with his buddies, have coffee, play cards or golf pushed him over the edge. I also lost a "special" lady friend who decided, because of the pandemic, to move to Florida and live with her family. I do miss her companionship.

The lady next door is a real character, always telling me, "People are no damn good," when she talked about the news. In particular, she dislikes politicians, telling me she would not be my friend if I ran for political office. She always told me about all her health problems, including the fact that she suffered from severe migraine headaches. She explained, "It's like sitting at a train crossing with the flashing of the lights, the clanging of the bell, and the roar of the train passing." She said it just kept going and going, and seemed like there was no end to the train.

Sometime after the pandemic began, she called me on the phone and told me to open my garage door, which I did. Shortly after, she pulled into my driveway and placed two large packages of toilet paper in my garage; this occurred several times with more toilet paper, as well as paper towels, powdered milk, canned food, etc. She was hoarding so much stuff in her own garage that she had no room for her car.

We have a retired science professor in the neighborhood who I like. I admire his beautiful, perfectly white, manicured beard and mustache. He always wears a cardigan sweater and has a pipe in his hand, which I am not sure he ever smokes; at least, I have never seen any smoke coming from it. During the pandemic, he kept us all informed on the neighborhood Facebook page about the latest scientific and medical data. He would always finish with a quote saying, "Science will lead us out of this dilemma." He was not happy about how the government was handling the situation, and commented, "Those guys don't know the difference between poop and chocolate. They need to stay out of it and leave the scientists alone to solve the problem. But no, they continue to screw things up."

I had always picked up my prescriptions at the drug store, but during the pandemic I had them delivered as everyone else in the neighborhood did. Well, one morning the neighbor lady called and asked if I had received a delivery from the drugstore. I said yes and that the medication was on my bathroom counter. She asked if I would please check it because she had mistakenly received mine. Sure enough, I had hers. I told her I would walk over to her house and make the exchange. She asked if she should call the doctor because she had taken one of my dark green capsules. I told her I did not think that was dangerous since it was just an eye vitamin. Wow, I wonder what would have happened if it had been Viagra!!

And then, of course, there were those damn masks. If we needed to venture out, we were required to wear masks. I wouldn't say I liked those masks; it was hard to breathe and talk. I purchased a package of masks and kept some in the car and others in my coat pockets so they were readily available. When stores and businesses began to reopen, you were still required to wear a mask, even in a restaurant. As I've said, it was challenging to eat and drink. I remember receiving a reminder from my doctor about my annual "wellness test" and that a mask would be required. It also stated that if I was sick then I should not come to the office. What? Other than checkups, isn't that why you go to the doctor? Isn't it because you don't feel well? The other day, I went to a Chinese restaurant for lunch, and all the staff were still wearing masks. Glad I don't work there.

The pandemic changed the way we shopped. We ordered online, and the store would bring it to our car in the parking lot, limiting our exposure to people. The delivery person wore a mask, and we usually wore a mask. They typically placed the merchandise in the trunk or back of the car. Or we could have it delivered by DoorDash, GrubHub, InstaCart, or another delivery service. This service sprang up all over, and most still exist. And, of course, Amazon thrived and still does. Retail stores and shops continue to struggle to reclaim their market share. In a way, it is unfortunate.

Yes, the pandemic changed our lives. It also cost us about two years of our lives, and at my age, I didn't have two years to give. Young people lost the most experiences, and they will never be able to recover. In addition to losing educational opportunities, they lost all the joy of being young—school ball games, field trips, proms, graduations, parties, dances, etc. There were weddings without guests, as well as honeymoons and vacations canceled because resorts and hotels were closed. How about the people who could not visit family members in the hospital? They could not be with them when they died, and then they could not have a funeral to honor their memory. And, of course, the churches were closed, so we could not participate in our usual religious beliefs.

Okay, so we survived the pandemic. We lived through it and allowed it to change our lives. Things will never be the same. It proved one thing to me: we are at the mercy of our leaders; they can take our freedom in a heartbeat. Think about it. They told us exactly what we could and could not do. Sometimes, we could be fined or jailed if we did not comply. Did our leaders, politicians, and healthcare officials learn from the experience? Did we learn from the experience? Did we over or under react?

Dammit, I hope it never happens again in my or anyone's lifetime. We should be able to live our lives!!

*"I have heard that the first sign of COVID is bad taste.
In reviewing this book,
it appears I've been infected for a long time."*

- Thomas L. Rose

Dammit!

"Well done is better than well said."
-Benjamin Franklin

Dammit Dolls

The image on the front cover is a *Handmade PinonyHead Dammit Doll* created by La Dame Creates, which is located in Loveland, Colorado.

Sometimes you want to yell,
when things are not going well.
That is when you need a Dammit Doll.
One that you can throw at the wall,
or just toss it down the hall.
Don't tear out your hair,
Just beat it on your chair.
And every time you slam it,
yell Dammit, Dammit, Dammit!!

When writing this book, I used my PinonyHead Dammit Doll quite a few times. It really, really helped relieve my stress and it will help you too.

Tom

Get your doll at:
www.ladamecreates.com

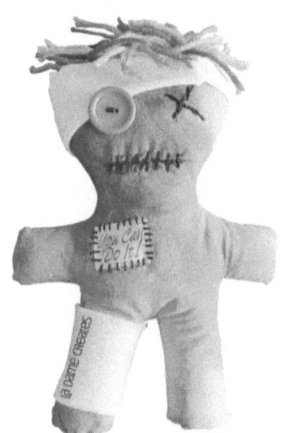

Dammit!

"Wish not so much to live long as to live well."
-Benjamin Franklin

About the Author

Thomas L. Rose, Tom Rose, was born in Peru, Indiana, November 21, 1940, to Norman and Donna (Hipskind) Rose. He has two younger sisters Jacquelyn (Rose) Roberts (deceased) and Jill (Rose) England.

The family moved from Peru to Goshen, Indiana, where he still resides. He attended St. John's Parochial School and Goshen High School graduating in 1958. He attended St. Joseph, Ball State and Goshen College.

He married Joyce Grissom in 1962. Their son, Brock, was born in 1964. Brock and his wife, Rose, have a daughter Amanda.

Tom worked in advertising and marketing most of his life and actually still does today with his son, Rose and Rose Associates.

With his wife Joyce he co-authored two cookbooks, *Cooking Together Chinese Style* and *Cooking Together Quick and Easy*. They also hosted a cooking segment on the local Fox TV affiliate for 13 years. During that time, they toured the Midwest teaching cooking classes.

After his wife's death Tom, with help from his son, authored a third cookbook, *Cooking Together Revisited*, which is dedicated to Joyce with the proceeds going to the families of Breast Cancer Support Projects.

Shortly after publication of the cookbook a friend, after reading Tom's grief journal notes, urged him to write a book about his grief journey. The book, *Balloon in A Box: Coping with Grief,* was released in the spring of 2021 with a second, updated edition in the summer of 2023.

As Tom says, "With that little book I caught lightning in a bottle because I suddenly became an author and a speaker. Since releasing the book, I have made over 135 speaking appearances at churches, service clubs, retirement communities and even prisons. The experience has brought me closer to my faith and has resulted in significant life changes."

In the spring of 2023, he published a murder mystery novel, *The Secret is in the Pasta*, and in 2024 he began hosting Senior Talk Michiana, a podcast featuring interviews with senior organizations, services and events in the Michiana area. Tom, along with his family, produce a YouTube cooking show, Cooking Together Generations, to help promote their Breast Cancer Support Projects.

In addition to cooking Tom enjoys playing golf and listening to music, all kinds. He takes great pleasure in cooking with the family and cooking for friends. Asked about the future he answered, "At 83 years old you are not really sure how much time you have left but I hope that I can keep working on my podcast and making speaking appearance with my *Balloon in A Box* book. I also have lot of ideas and would like to write more books, but that is all in God's hands."

Note from the Author

Thank you for taking the time to read this book, and I would love for you to share your thoughts and opinions. Check my website:

www.ThomasLRose.com

and

www.cookingtogether.com

Or email me at:

roseandrose@comcast.net

It All Began With

After the death of his wife, encouraged by a friend, Tom wrote a book, *Balloon in A Box: Coping with Grief.* With that little book, as he says, "I caught lightning in a bottle because I suddenly became an author and a speaker." Since releasing the book in the spring of 2021 and a second edition in 2023. Tom has made over 160 speaking appearances to audiences ranging from 8 to 300 at churches, service clubs, retirement communities, corporate meetings, and even prisons.

If you would be interested in having him as a speaker for your organization, please contact him at:

Tel: 574-596-6256

or

E-mail: roseandrose@comcast.net

The book is available on Amazon and at:

www.thomaslrose.com

And Then

Encouraged by the success of *Balloon in A Box*, Tom decided to challenge his writing ability by authoring a murder mystery. So then came *The Secret is in the Pasta*, a murder mystery that takes place in an Italian restaurant. Tom says, "Writing the novel was great fun, especially creating the characters." Sometime in the future, he hopes to write a sequel to the continuing story.

The book is available on Amazon and at:

www.thomaslrose.com

"Many of life's failures are people who did not realize how close they were to success when they gave up."

-Thomas Edison

And Now

SENIOR TALK
Resources Podcast

Not over the Hill Yet! Tom has taken the opportunity to host a podcast, Senior Talk Michiana. Stemming from his speaking appearances at senior communities, he became involved with the senior organizations in Michiana (Southern Michigan and Northern Indiana).

Senior Talk Michiana is a weekly podcast dedicated to empowering seniors by providing them with essential information about services, organizations, and events throughout the Michiana area.

Our mission is to serve as a voice for seniors, addressing the issues that impact their lives. We are committed to delivering high-quality information from reputable senior service providers and organizations, ensuring that all seniors have access to the resources available to them. Our goal is to enhance quality of life and to advocate for the dignity and respect they deserve.

Available at:

Senior Talk Michiana on Spotify

www.seniortalkmichiana.org

www.thomaslrose.com/senior-talk